Music Activity Book

Ellen J. McHenry

DOVER PUBLICATIONS
Garden City, New York

Note

This book is filled with games, puzzles, secret codes, coloring pages, mazes and lots more—and they're all about music, musicians and musical instruments of all sorts. After you've worked the puzzles and such, you can check your answers in the Solutions section beginning on page 41.

Bibliographical Note

Music Activity Book is a new work, first published by Dover Publications in 1996.

International Standard Book Number
ISBN-13: 978-0-486-29079-9
ISBN-10: 0-486-29079-4

Manufactured in the United States of America
29079419
www.doverpublications.com

This happy violinist is about to have some surprises! Can you circle the <u>four</u> things that don't belong in this picture?

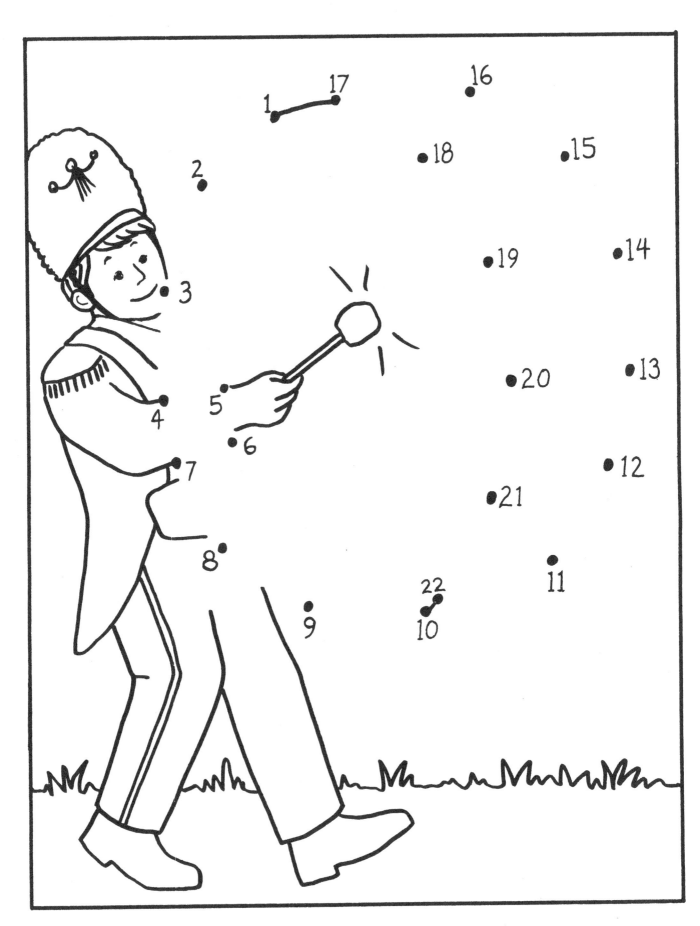

What big, loud instrument is this young fellow playing? Connect the dots to find out!

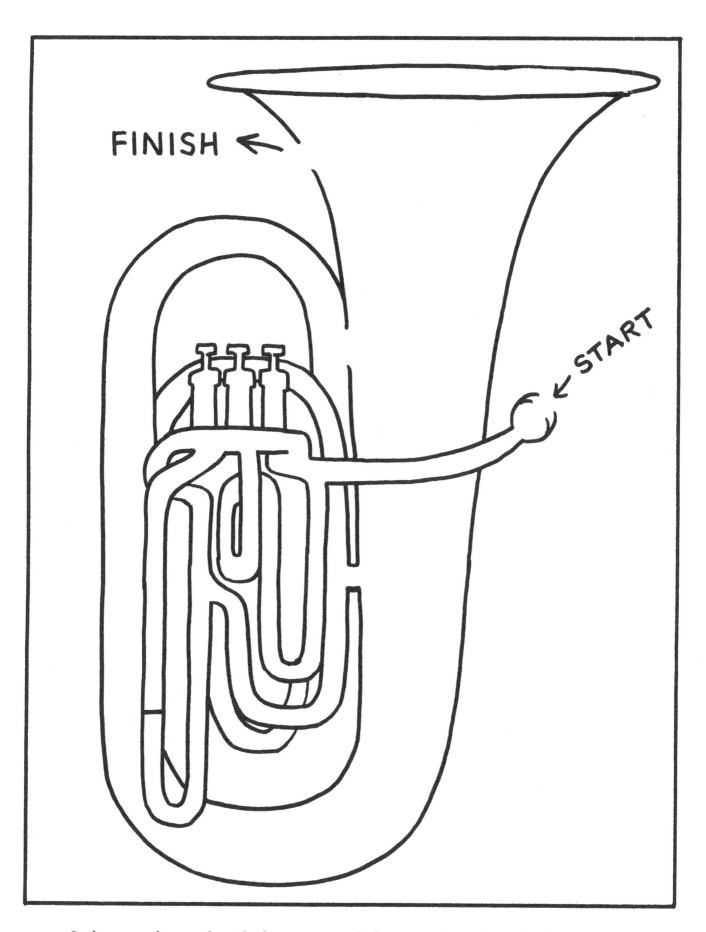

FINISH ←

← START

In this unusual maze of metal tubing, you must find your way through the tuba, from START to FINISH. You're allowed to go *under* or *over* any tube to get out.

C	B	M	S	P	N	L
T	A	S	N	A	R	E
S	Y	C	T	Q	I	A
D	L	M	I	E	G	U
B	R	L	P	N	D	J
O	E	T	O	A	B	Z
N	H	C	G	W	N	R
G	T	Y	C	L	G	I
O	F	B	A	S	S	H

The <u>five</u> names of drums on the facing page are hidden somewhere in this puzzle. Can you find their names there and circle each one? You can go across, down or slantwise in any direction.

Did you ever dance the Cha-Cha? Hidden in this picture is a pair of very popular Latin-American instruments used in this dance. You can find them by coloring the picture according to these numbers: 1 = red   2 = blue   3 = green   4 = white   5 = yellow

6

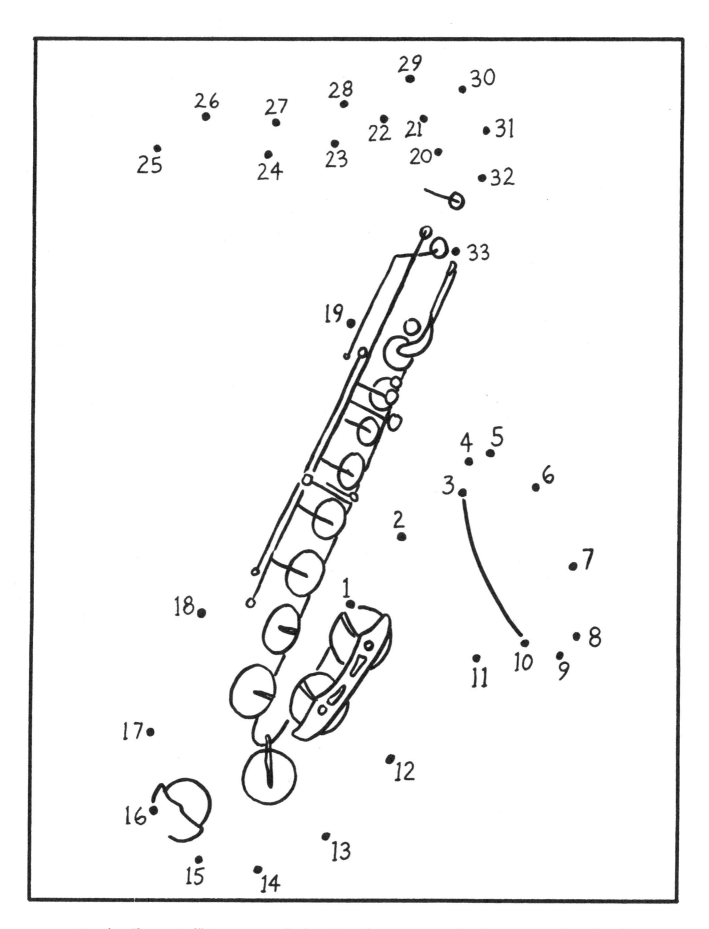

Here's a "brasswind" instrument that's right at home in a jazz band or in a marching band. Connect the dots to find out what it is!

On this page and the next there's a relaxed young fellow enjoying his music. But a *lot* of changes are going on while he plays. Can you circle the <u>nine</u> differences between these two pictures?

The music at the top of this page tells us all the note names, from **E** up to **D**. Use this "secret code" to fill in the missing names of the <u>two</u> common objects at the bottom.

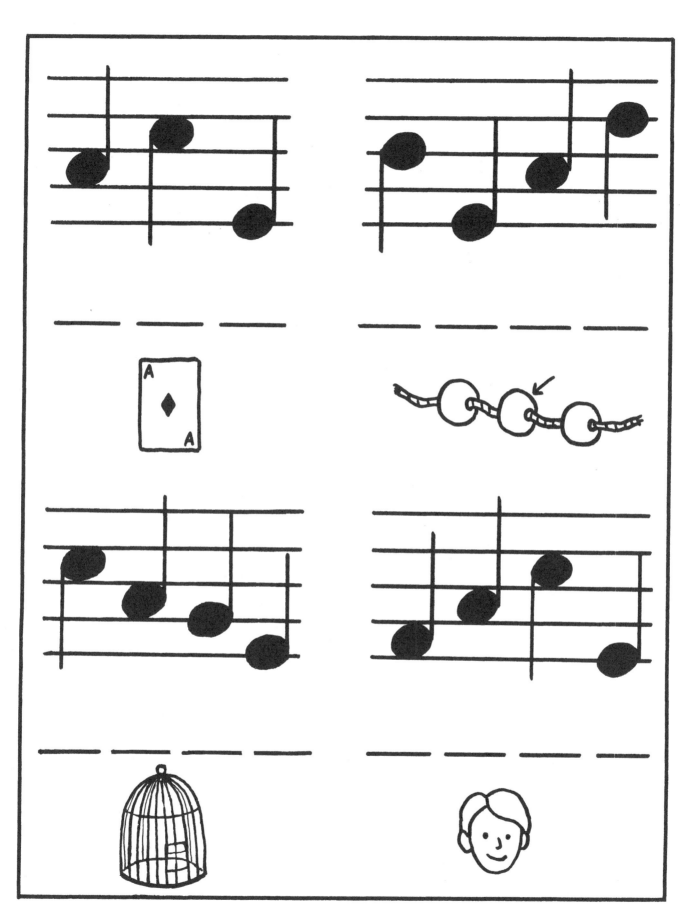

Use the same "secret code" as before to fill in the missing names of these <u>four</u> objects.

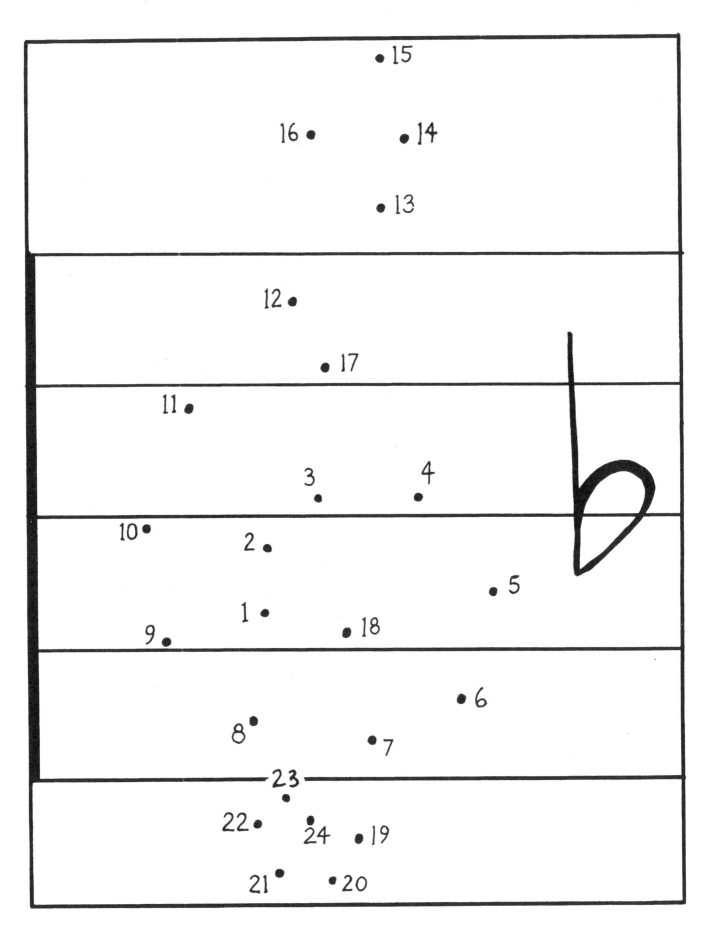

The music sign on the right is a "flat." But next to it is a *hidden* sign you'll need if you want to read music. Connect those dots to find out what it is!

This noisy fellow is ready to wake up everybody at camp! But the surprise is on him! Can you circle the <u>seven</u> things that don't belong in this picture?

This guitarist is ready to rock 'n' roll. But he's sure going to need his loudspeaker if he wants to be heard. You can help him make sure he's connected by drawing a line all along that wire, starting at the guitar.

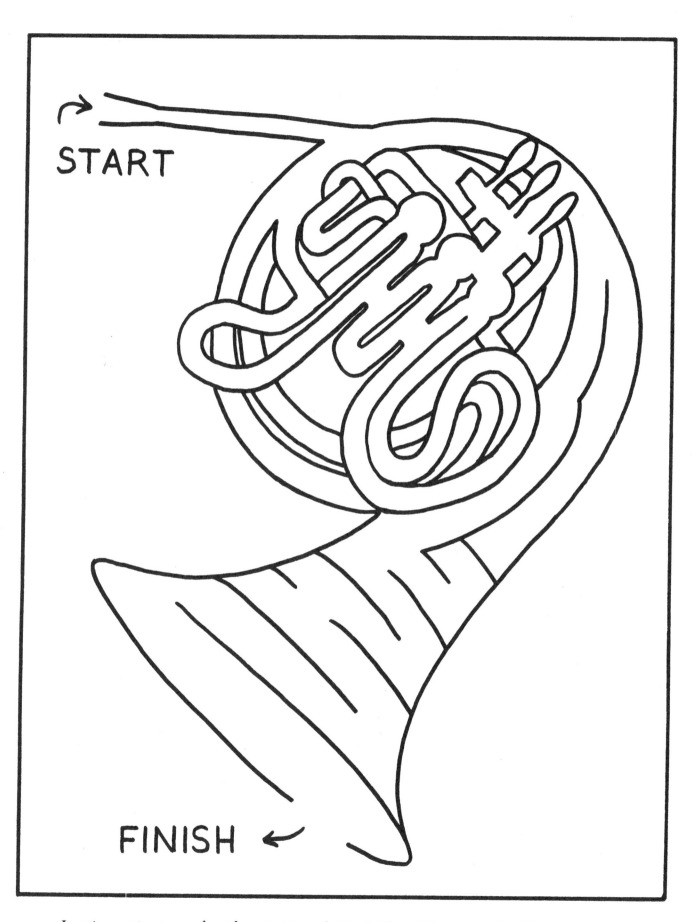

Imagine getting trapped inside a giant French Horn! What a job to get out! But there is a way to travel from START to FINISH. Can you draw a line to show the way out? You're allowed to go *under* or *over* any tube.

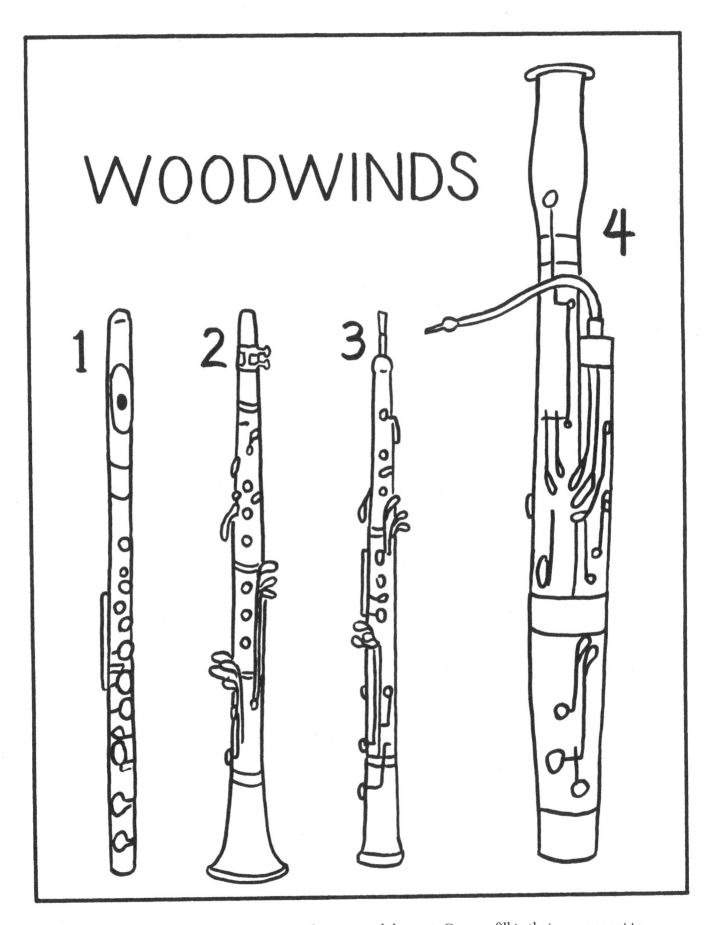

WOODWINDS

Look at the <u>five</u> wind instruments on this page and the next. Can you fill in their names next to their numbers in the crossword puzzle? (*Here's a hint to get started: "Number 1 down" begins with* F-L-U...) Number 5 is a popular short form of the instrument's name.

What are these two guys up to? Even while playing their instruments, they've hidden <u>eight</u> music notes like this one ♪ on their bodies. Can you find them and circle them?

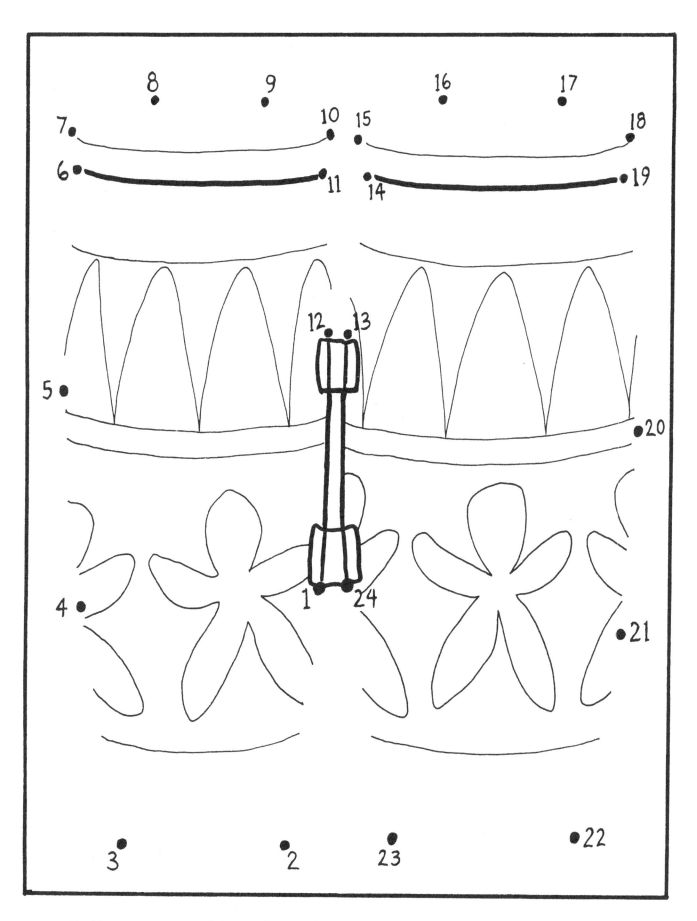

You'll want to get up and dance when you hear the sounds of these two percussion instruments!
Connect the dots to find out what they look like.

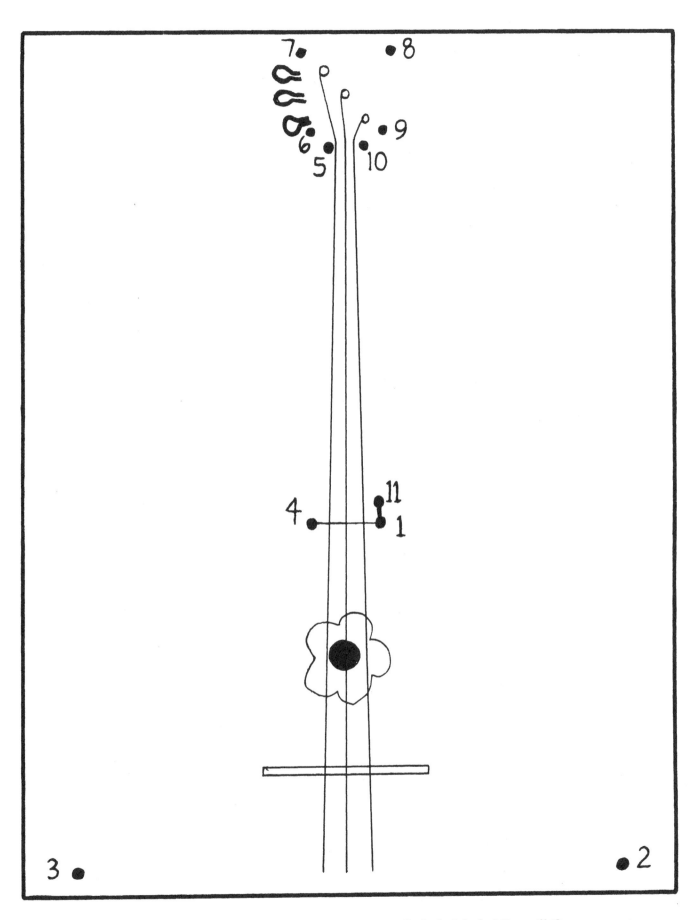

Have you ever seen the three-stringed Russian guitar called a *balalaika*? You will if you connect the dots.

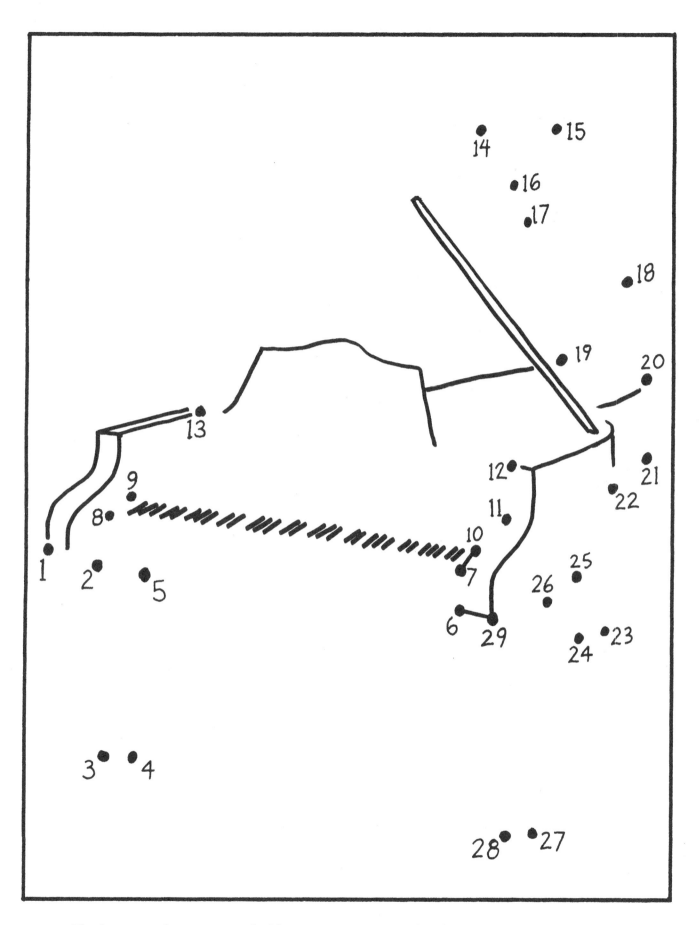

This heavyweight instrument had better get some strong legs before it falls on the floor! And while you're at it, how about a lid to keep out the rain? Just connect the dots to complete the picture.

"*Mary, Mary, quite contrary, How does your garden grow?*" This time, Mary is watering a very funny-looking bunch of flowers. (And what's that she's holding in her right hand?) . . . .

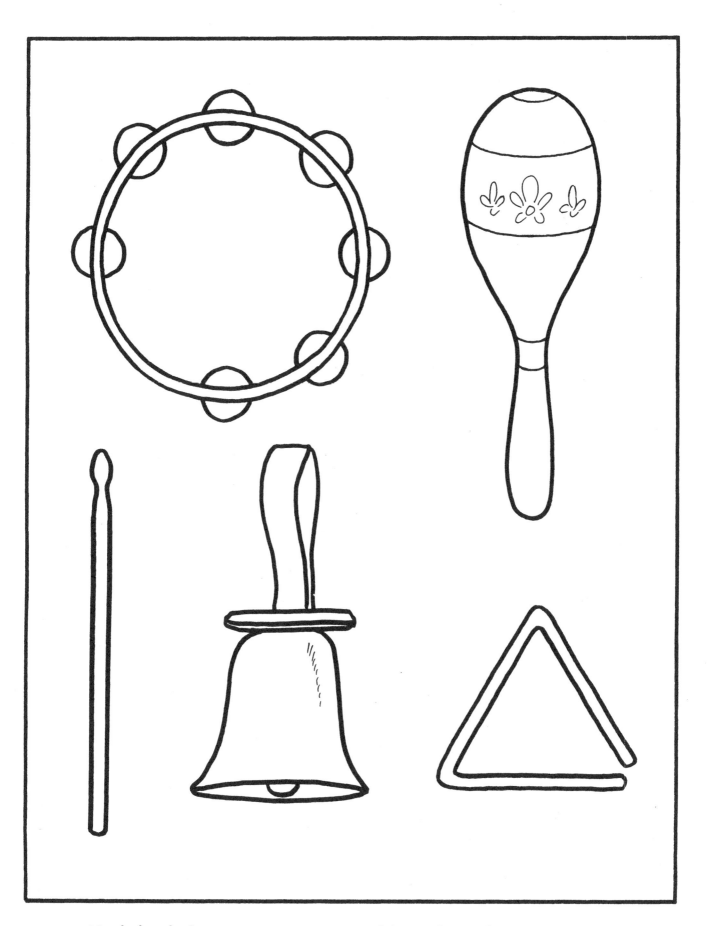

. . . . Now look at the <u>four</u> percussion instruments and the <u>one</u> drumstick on this page. Can you draw a long line connecting each object to its duplicate in Mary's garden?

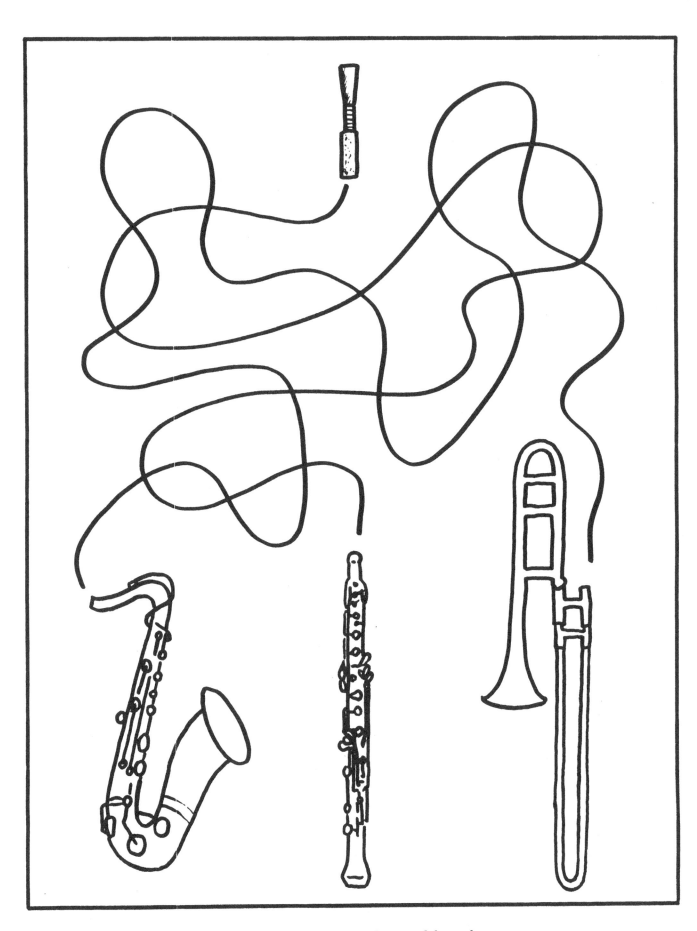

The reed mouthpiece at the top of the page fits only one of these three instruments.
Is it the <u>saxophone</u>, on the left? Or the <u>oboe</u>, in the middle? Or the <u>trombone</u>, on the right?
Follow the wiggly line from the mouthpiece to find the answer.

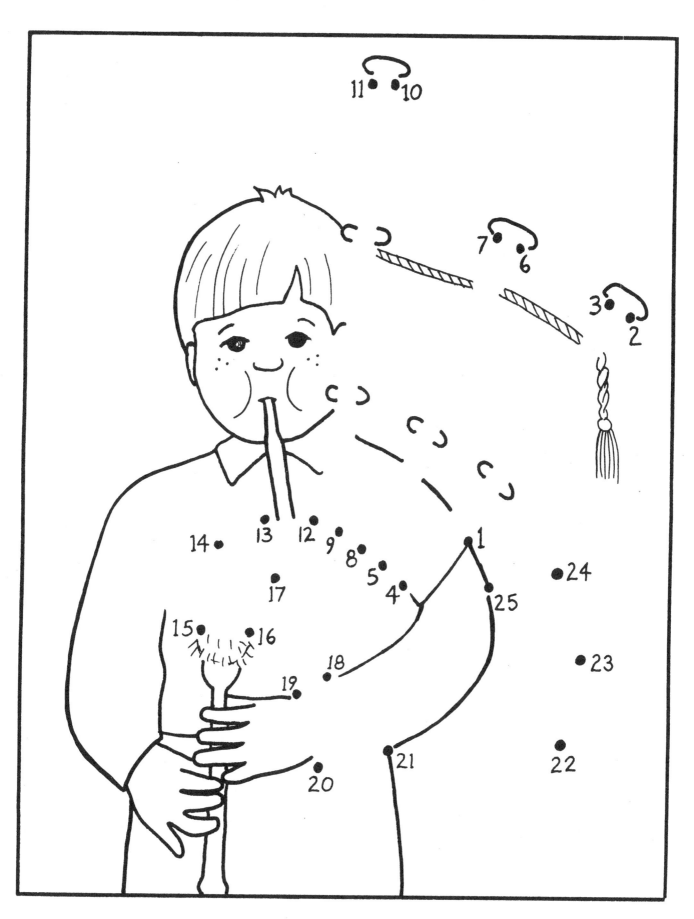

Could this be the famous *"Tom, Tom, the piper's son"*? If it is, help him play his invisible instrument by connecting the dots.

These <u>five</u> names of string instruments are well hidden somewhere in the puzzle on the facing page. Can you find all five names and circle them? You can go across, down or slantwise in any direction.

B	N	E	H	A	R	P
T	G	V	I	O	L	A
C	U	H	G	D	S	V
F	I	L	C	A	J	N
W	T	B	Y	T	I	C
S	A	M	A	L	K	E
E	R	H	O	N	C	L
Y	T	I	D	S	M	L
S	V	G	L	P	R	O

That boy better catch the rascally squirrel if he's going to play his drum with that stolen drumstick! Help him find his way by drawing a line between him and that tricky little animal.

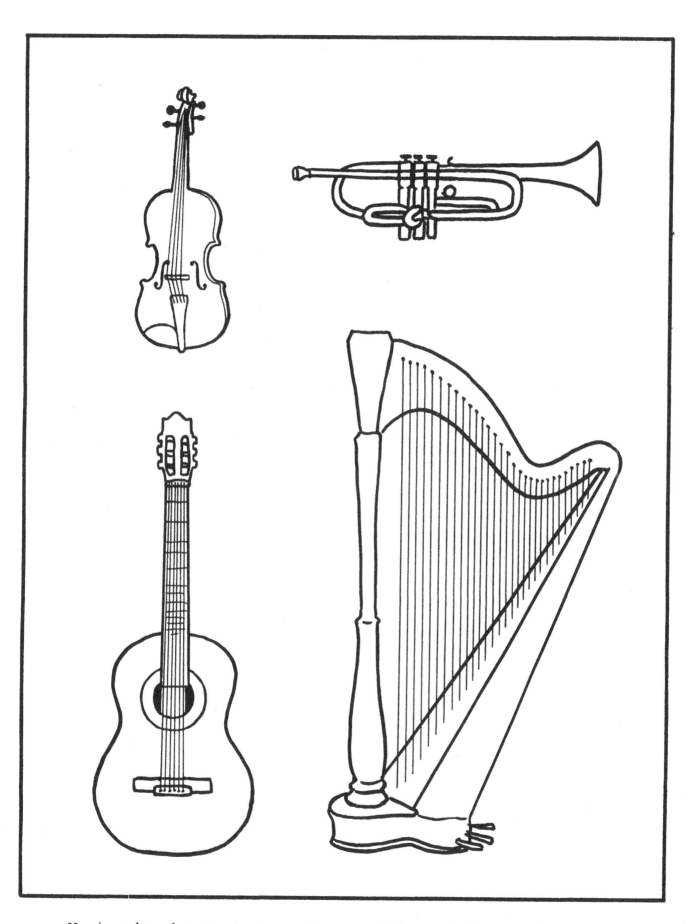

Here's a violin and a trumpet on top ... and a guitar and a harp on the bottom. Only one of these instruments <u>doesn't</u> <u>need</u> <u>strings</u> to make its sound. Can you circle that instrument?

What do you call it when only *one* person sings? Or *four* people? Or *eight*?! The answers are hidden by that fantastic secret code on the facing page...

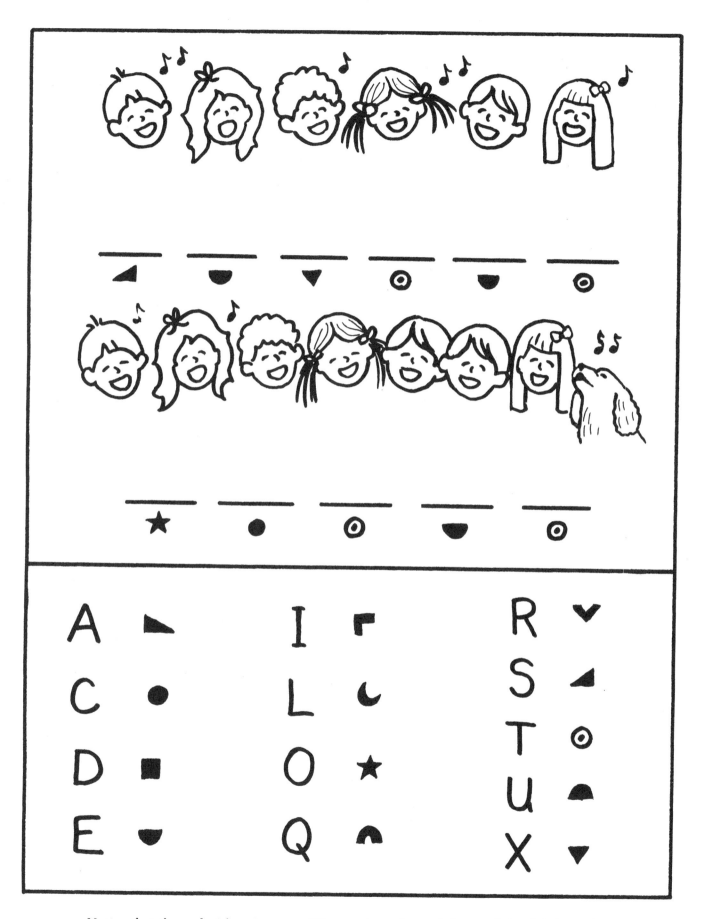

... Notice that the code (above) uses a different shape for each letter of the alphabet—like a *square* for a "D" and a *star* for an "O." Can you solve the mystery, and fill in the <u>six</u> missing words?

On this page and the next, the marching boy and his friends are having a great time at the parade. (Only the dog doesn't like the noise!) But a *lot* of changes are going on while the boy plays! Can you circle the <u>ten</u> differences between these two pictures?

33

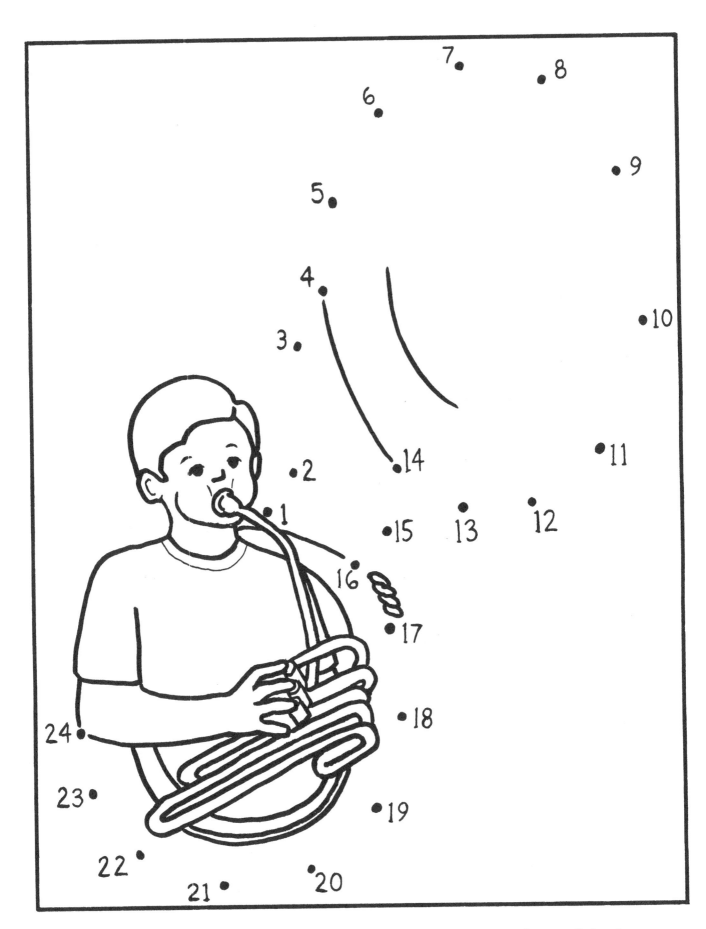

"OOm-pah OOm-pah" goes this great big brass instrument. But where is the rest of it? Help us find the missing parts by connecting the dots.

Poor John has lost one of his cymbals at the other end of the field. Can you help him find it before the marching band needs him to play? Hurry to draw a line between John and that missing cymbal!

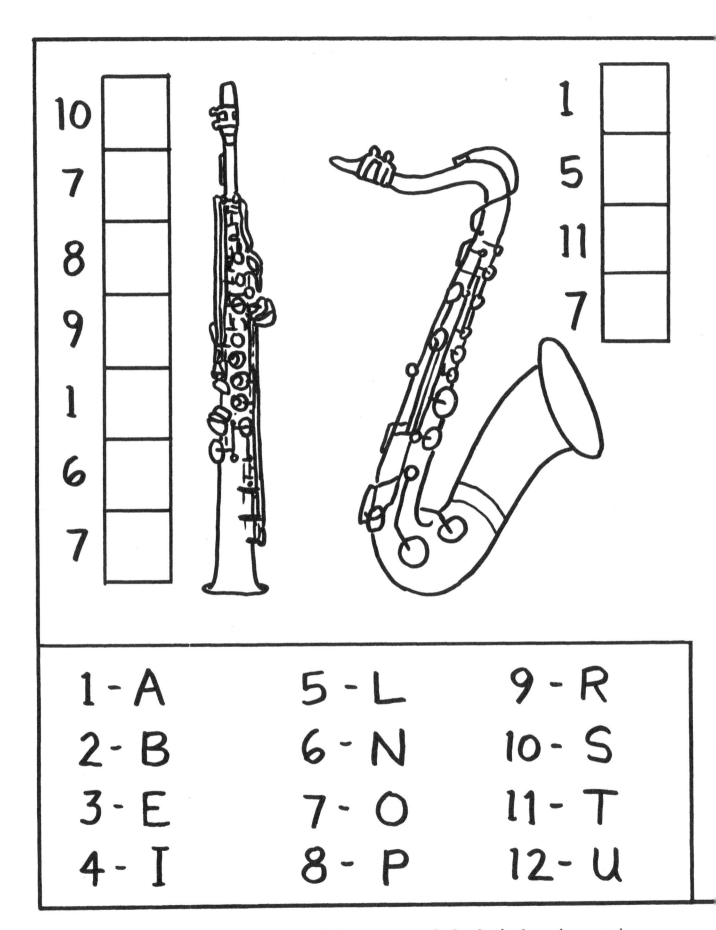

1 - A   5 - L   9 - R

2 - B   6 - N   10 - S

3 - E   7 - O   11 - T

4 - I   8 - P   12 - U

Here's a code that uses numbers instead of letters to name the <u>four</u> kinds of saxophones on these two pages. Just fill in the right letter next to its matching number. To get started in the first picture, try the letter **S** next to "10" and **O** next to "7." Now figure out the rest!

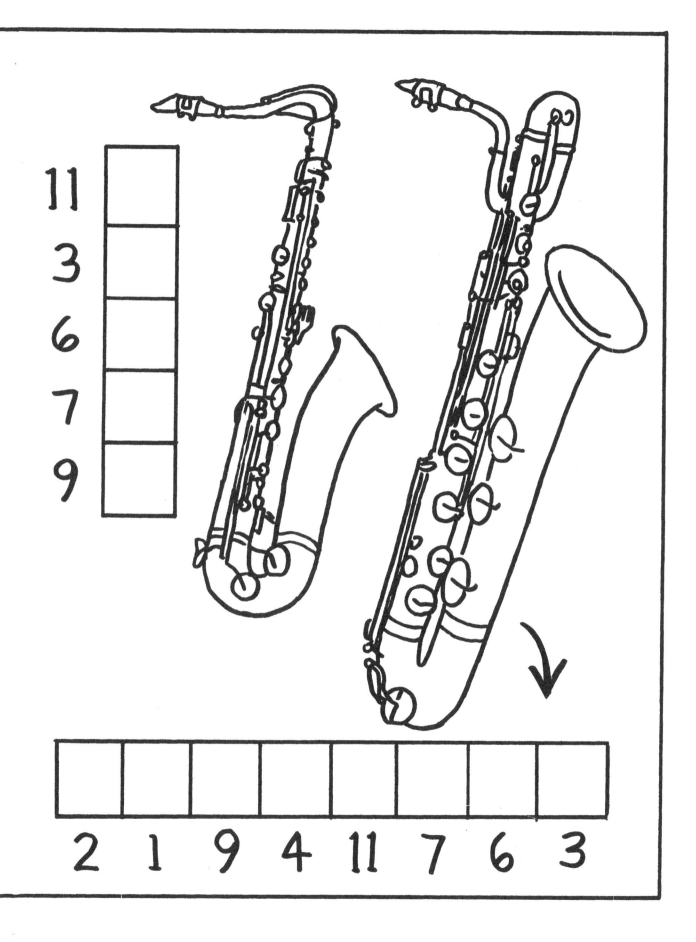

The four musicians on this page can't play a note because their instruments are missing!!! Where are they? Why, right on the facing page! Your job is to assign the right instrument to the right player...

☐ Scottish bagpipe

☐ Indian pungi

☐ African drum

☐ Spanish castanets

... Do this by filling in the letter **A**, **B**, **C** or **D** in the empty box next to each instrument. To get started, which musician can't make a sound without his or her SCOTTISH BAGPIPE? Is it musician **A**, **B**, **C** or **D**?

Poor Billy is just too far away from his music to know *what* to play. (He should have memorized the piece!) Can you help him? You can save the day—and the concert—by drawing a line between Billy and his faraway music stand.

Solutions

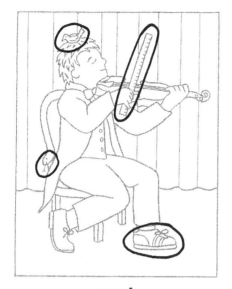

page 1

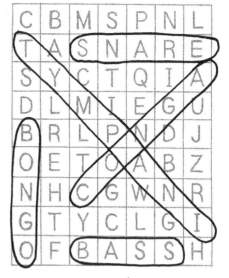

page 4

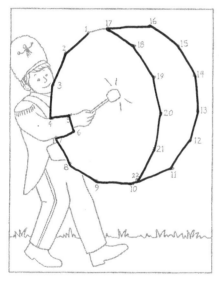

page 2

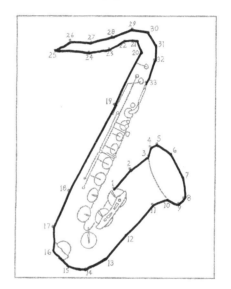

page 7

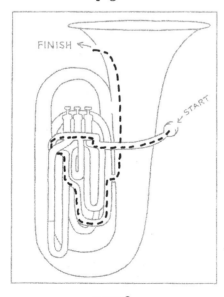

page 3

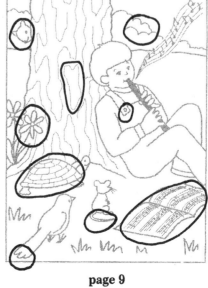

page 9

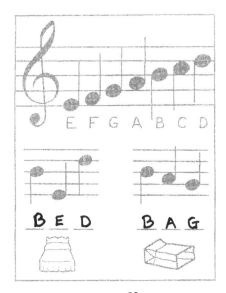

page 10

page 13

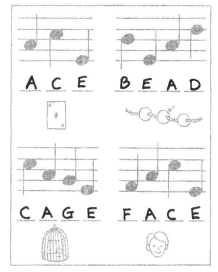

page 11

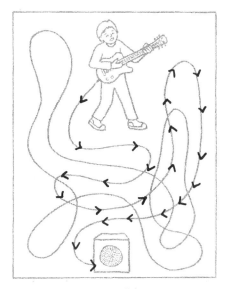

page 14

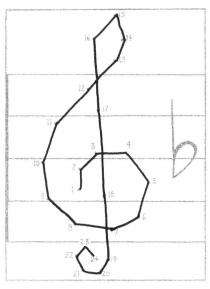

page 12

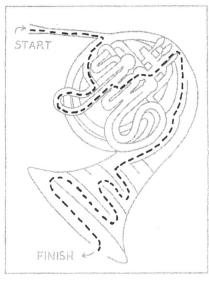

page 15

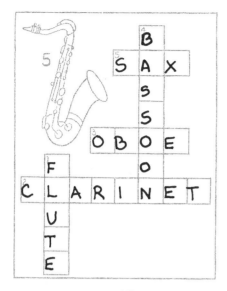

page 17

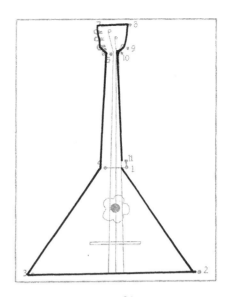

page 20

page 18

page 21

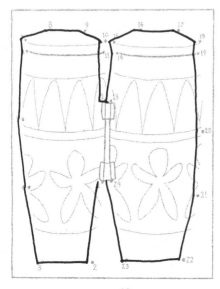

page 19

page 22

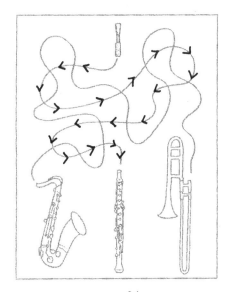

page 24

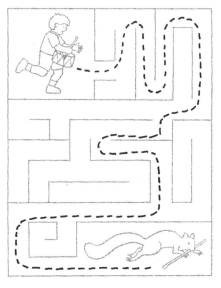

page 28

page 25

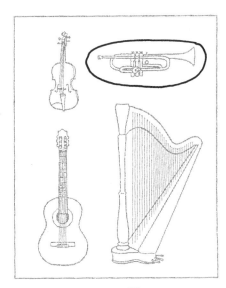

page 29

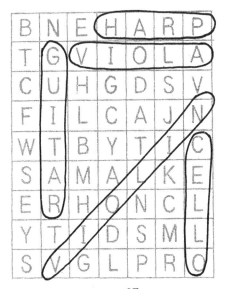

page 27

page 30

page 31

page 33

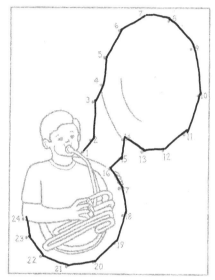

page 34

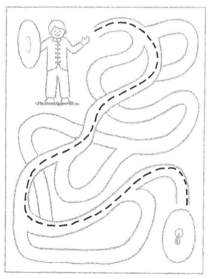

page 35

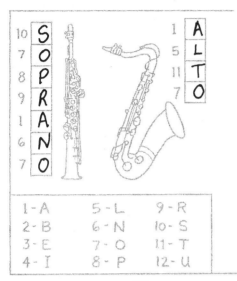

page 36

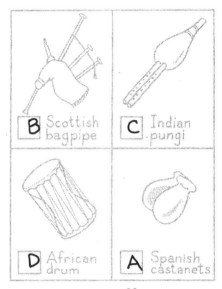

page 39

page 37

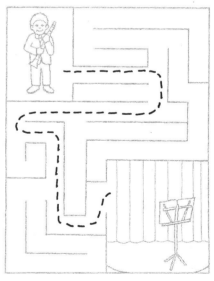

page 40